Snooze

A HELPFUL GUIDE FOR SLEEPY OWLS

by

Eilidh Muldoon

Feeling tired after a busy day?

But you can't sleep?

Then **Snooze** is the perfect book for you!

It will explain how to get the **best sleep ever.**

Find somewhere peaceful,

and make sure you are **nice and comfortable.**

Honk!

It's very important that **you're not disturbed.**

honk
HONK! HONK
honk
Honk
HONK
HONK
HONK
HONK
honk?
Honk
HONK
HONK!
HONK! HOnk.
Honk!

Now

snuggle

down...

...and enjoy the wonderful **peace and quiet.**

COCK-A-DOODLE **DOO!**

It is always best to
keep the lights off.

We sleep so much better in the dark.

Sometimes it helps to listen to something **soothing** – a lullaby, or the whisper of a breeze in the leaves.

But nothing **too loud**
or raucous.

Sometimes neighbours don't realise that you're trying to sleep, so just ask them – very politely – **to keep the noise down.**

By now...

...you will be

cosy...

...and **relaxed.**

Ready
for the
best
sleep
ever.

Close your eyes...
and soon you'll
be **sound asleep,**
without a care
in the world.

SNORE!!

If you follow these **simple steps** you will wake up rested, refreshed and ready for a brand new day.

Perhaps your friends would like to borrow this book.

After all,
everyone needs
a good night's sleep!